ZEEKA'S GHOST

REVENGE OF ZEEKA

BOOK FOUR

AUTHOR BRENDA MOHAMMED

CONTENTS

INTRODUCTION 4

ZEEKA'S GHOST: BOOK 4 6

A BROKEN URN..................................6

STORMY WEATHER 14

STRANGER CLEARS ROAD 18

ASHES DISAPPEAR...........................22

STEVEN SEES APPARITION 26

ZEEKA'S GHOST APPEARS 31

STEVEN TELLS RAYNOR...................36

GHOST WARNS STEVEN 41

STEVEN IS HONOURED 45

STEVEN IS INTERVIEWED 50

MANDY DISAPPEARS.......................56

JACK AND JERRY INTERVENE...........61
MANDY WAS KIDNAPPED 65
STEVEN IS IN DANGER 69
GHOST STOPS KIDNAPPERS 72
STEVEN FORGIVES ZEEKA 75
ZEEKA CHRONICLES 78
ZEEKA AND THE ZOMBIES II............81
REVENGE OF ZEEKA HORROR
TRILOGY 84
RESURRECTION 87
AUTHOR BIOGRAPHY 90
BOOKS BY AUTHOR.........................97
COPYRIGHT NOTICE 106

INTRODUCTION

The drama of the Zeeka Series continues in Zeeka's Ghost: Revenge of Zeeka Book 4. The book is the fourth installment in the five-book Science Fiction series, Revenge of Zeeka, and can be read as a standalone.

Dr. Steven Sharpe is engrossed in inventing a miracle cure for Alzheimer's disease.

Unknown to him he and his wife Mandy are targets of enemies.

Their lives may be at stake.

Steven must find a way to hunt down and apprehend ruthless kidnappers and save his beloved wife.

The sudden appearance of Zeeka's Ghost upsets Steven.

Does the ghost have evil intentions?

Is the ghost here to harm or help Steven and Mandy?

How will Steven deal with a ghost on one hand and kidnappers on the other?

Here is what a Reviewer said:

Extending from her Zeeka and the Zombies trilogy is Mohammed's most nostalgic offering, Zeeka's Ghost. Zeeka is back but not at all how you expect. Unresolved issues, regrets, and love are all splendidly woven together with the right mix of startling plot twists the author is masterful at. Fans of the series will not be disappointed and new fans will be caught up to speed in no time. Another thrilling read! [Amazon Reviewer]

ZEEKA'S GHOST: BOOK 4

A BROKEN URN

The inhabitants of the Isle of Gosh appeared to have long recovered from the horror that took place two years before when Zeeka and the Zombies had terrorized the island. The island's chief source of revenue was tourism, and tourists from all over the world flocked to the island to enjoy the white sandy beaches and fun entertainment areas.

However, did they forget? Three natives were conversing in a dimly lit bar in a secluded part of the beach. It was January 2038, and the bar still maintained the rustic appearance of thirty years ago, unlike the posh modern ones in the city. There were two empty bottles of scotch on the table next to an ashtray filled with cigarette butts. Their conversation was muffled. They huddled together speaking in hushed tones.

A perky waitress, in a bright red dress, smiled as she went up to them and asked, “Hey, my name’s Jean.
Would you like anything else?” Without looking at her, the burly-looking one waved his hand backward to send her away. She mumbled, “Bloody drunkards. Can’t expect a tip from them.”
She stopped at an adjacent table to pick up the empty glasses and eavesdropped on part of their conversation. One of them was saying to the other two, “Those zombies killed my brother in a horrific way. His wife received money from the proceeds of Zeeka’s estate.
What about me? What do I get for losing a brother? Did they think to throw a bit of money her way was fair compensation? They should be made to pay more.”
“Criminals,” Jean muttered as she walked away.
Newlyweds, Steven and Mandy, relaxed on the leather reclining chairs in the living room of their brand new home with outstanding views of the sea. The sound of the waves lashing against the shore was most soothing to their ears.

They were discussing how lucky they were to get their posh island villa at a bargain price, just a couple blocks away from Mandy's sister, Janet, and Raynor, Steven's brother. The upper floor of the house had three bedrooms, each with its private bathroom, and a large wrap - around porch. The kitchen, living room, dining room, utility area, and a vast study area were on the lower floor. There were living quarters for a helper adjoining the house. An elevator connected the upper floor with the ground floor, but there were also steps, in the event of a power cut.

Steven and Mandy were a loving couple with many shared interests. Steven was in charge of medical research at Gosh Central Hospital, and Mandy was a part-time nurse. Neither one could conceive, but they were not disturbed about that.

Ophelia, the brilliant two-year-old daughter of Janet and Raynor, frequented their home. She had grown into an adorable little girl, with peachy skin, dark brown hair, and dark brown eyes. They loved her, and she loved her aunt and uncle. Whenever Janet and Raynor needed a babysitter, both Steven

and Mandy volunteered if they were available. They loved to read stories to her and watch her fall asleep.
While dozing off in each other's arms, there was a knock on the door. Mandy jumped up to see who it was. It was Janet's helper, Miranda, a robot, holding Ophelia's hand.
Miranda said, "Mandy, can you keep Ophelia here for a short while until I finish my chores? Janet and Raynor are at the hospital."
"Sure," said Mandy. "Steven and I are not planning to go anywhere today. It's not a public holiday, but we have some time off. We'd keep her."
On hearing that, Ophelia ran into Mandy's arms and said, "Aunt Mandy, will you tell me the story of Hurricane Katrina?"
"I will, Ophelia," Mandy said, as she hugged her close to her.
"Do you know that is a real event? It happened thirty-three years ago. I was a little girl like you when that hurricane destroyed New Orleans."
Miranda thanked Mandy and left. Mandy took Ophelia into the study.

The large study had two state-of-the-art computers and bookshelves with Steven's favorite books on Medicine and Technology. A few of Mandy's favorite books, which she had read several times, were also displayed. She cherished those books. Mandy was a fan of horror and other genres. She had a wide variety of books for adults and children by many famous authors.

Close to the window, there was a shelf with paraphernalia and an urn containing ashes. Mandy always meant to ask Steven to do something about the ashes in the urn. Whenever she saw it, it brought back memories of Zeeka and the Zombies. Although she was not present physically at the time they wreaked havoc on the island, she had seen it all on the daily television news.

There were two large comfortable couches in the room, and sometimes Mandy and Steven would relax on them, and read a book or two.

Ophelia pointed to a book on the shelf and said, "Aunt Mandy, can you read me that book please?" Mandy turned to the shelf,

took the book down and looked at it. The name was 'The Ghost of Normandy Road,' by John Hennessy. She said, "Ophelia darling, this book is not for kids. It is a horror story. I cannot read this book to you."
Ophelia pointed to another. Mandy checked, and it was "Sam's Song," by Hannah Howe. Mandy chuckled and said, "Ophelia, these books are for grown-ups.

Let me get you "Snow-white and the Seven Dwarfs."

She looked around. She could not see Ophelia. The window was open. "Ophelia, where are you?" she called out. At that moment, Steven walked in laughing. "There she is," he said. "She is behind the curtain."
Ophelia giggled, pushed the curtain aside, and ran out from her hiding place. A strong breeze blew. The curtain rose in the air and brought down the urn with extreme force. There was a loud crash, the urn broke, and ashes scattered on the floor.
The wind howled viciously. There were flashes of lightning and then loud thunder. Steven said to Mandy, "It seems like the storm is approaching. I heard the warning on the news last night but forgot to mention

it to you. You were asleep. I thought it would bypass the island. Storms always avoid this island, but maybe not this time. We should be grateful that it's not a hurricane."
He tried running to the window to close it, but stopped, as the house plunged into darkness from a power cut. Ophelia screamed, and Mandy held on to her to comfort her. All lines of communication were cut off immediately.
The emergency light flickered for a while, giving Steven time to shut the window. However, darkness once again engulfed the house, and there was no time to clean up the ashes. They closed the door to the study and fumbled their way in the darkness to the living room.
Steven said to Mandy, "I cannot understand why these blackouts occur in these modern times. It is time for our Government to spend some money on installing proper equipment on infrastructure."
Mandy responded, "I read in the newspapers that it is in their budget for next year."
"I want my Mummy," squealed Ophelia.

“We cannot contact your Mummy, darling. The phone lines are dead. We cannot use any electronic equipment,” Mandy gently said to Ophelia.

“Aunt Mandy, I am scared. Please hug me.” She clutched on to Mandy as she said those words.

Mandy sang a song for Ophelia. The soft tones of the lullaby soothed Ophelia as she snuggled into Mandy's arms. The little girl's breathing gradually became deep and even, and her body slumped heavily against Mandy's chest.

As she gently placed the sleeping child on the couch beside her, a strange noise broke the silence. She listened as she tucked a blanket around Ophelia. It sounded like someone, or something, was moving around in the study. Mandy shivered. It was dark, and she did not want to go to find out what it was. She looked cautiously at Steven. His face mirrored her own. He had heard it too and seemed equally reluctant to investigate. He said, "Maybe the wind's playing tricks on us."

Mandy nodded in agreement.

Meanwhile, at Raynor and Janet's home, Miranda stood frozen in the kitchen. She was cutting vegetables, and her hand, which was holding the knife, remained suspended in the air. The power outage had affected her ability to move, although the power generator had kicked in.

At the hospital, life support systems failed for a couple of seconds until the generators started automatically. Doctors and nurses scurried along the hospital corridors to keep an eye on patients.

Dr. Brown was at the bank requesting a withdrawal from his account and the power outage occurred in the middle of his transaction.

The storm strengthened, and darkness covered the entire island, except for the frequent flashes of lightning, followed by horrendous peals of thunder.

It was impossible for anyone to drive his or her electric vehicle in the stormy weather. Security systems failed. The rain poured ceaselessly imprisoning people in their homes and trapping some in business places. The wind howled wildly like a pack of angry wolves. The horrifying noise grew louder as it buffeted through the swaying trees, bringing them crashing down and making the roads impassable.

Mandy wished that Ophelia would sleep through it all. However, Ophelia woke up and asked for her favorite teddy bear. Steven held her while Mandy fumbled her way in the darkness to the kitchen to get her baby bag. She could not find it and suddenly remembered that it was in the study. She called out to Steven to get it.

Not wanting to leave Ophelia alone, he took her with him and opened the door to the study. It was pitch black in there, but he felt his way around and found the bag. As he reached out to pick it up, it gravitated towards him, and he grabbed it and left the room. He knew that something strange had just happened, but he dismissed the thought from his mind.

There was no way for Mandy and Steven to communicate with anyone anywhere. Cell phones and cell towers were down too. It was like a nightmare, but Steven and Mandy hid their fear from little Ophelia. They pretended that all was well.

"Why is it so dark, Uncle Steven?" she asked.

"There was a power cut dear. It should be fixed in a few minutes," he answered softly.

"I'm scared," she said. "I want my Mummy and Daddy." She clutched on to him tightly.

“They’ll soon be home, and they’ll come for you, babe” he replied gently. Steven knew that would not be the case for a very long while as he handed her back to Mandy. Ophelia clutched her teddy bear tightly, snuggled up to Mandy, and eventually fell into a deep sleep.

STRANGER CLEARS ROAD

Dr. George Brown was still at the bank where the doors locked automatically, and no one could leave the building, which became shrouded in darkness. A staff member explained why the generators failed to work properly. It was the first time the bank was using them, and they did not perform as the manufacturers claimed they would.

Tempers flared. Some customers burst into arguments with each other and the bank staff, out of sheer frustration.

Persons needed funds to stock up on food supplies for their home because of the storm and were unable to access any of the automatic money dispensers in other parts of the island.

The bank manager approached the angry customers in an attempt to reassure them.

“There is a computer glitch. Our Head Office is working to resolve the problem. It will take a few minutes.”

“What’s the cause of this?” shouted an irate customer.

"Our main computer at the Computer Center crashed because of the storm, but we are getting a connection soon to the Central office where the backup files are held. Please be patient. I also advise that the bank would be closing for business in half an hour. Our staff needs to get home."
"I want money now," bellowed another angry customer.
At that stage, customers indulged in political discussions.
One said, "The Government has wasted this island's revenue.
They should have invested money many years ago in an emergency backup system for events like these."
Another replied, "You're right. Now the Prime Minister is telling us revenue is slow, and they have to cut expenditure. He's telling us to tighten our belts."
The storm eventually ceased, and power was restored. Customers calmed down. Some withdrew money at the Automatic teller machines, and others attempted to leave the bank, but as the rain was pouring heavily, some remained inside the building.

Dr. Brown decided to make a run for it, and dashed across the road in the pouring rain to where he had parked the car.
He got in, started it, and drove off.
On the way to the hospital, he was forced to bring the car to a halt. There were fallen trees across the road. As he parked there wondering what to do, a strange figure appeared from nowhere and moved aside some of the trees clearing a pathway for him. The rain was still pouring, and it did not seem to bother that individual.
He was muscular, was wearing a hooded jacket, and his face was hidden. As Dr. Brown re-started his car and looked around to thank the stranger, and perhaps offer him a lift somewhere, he could not see him. He had disappeared completely.
Was that man real? he wondered.
When he got to the hospital, he told Raynor about his experience. Raynor was puzzled and said, “Maybe he was a forest ranger doing some community service.
I expect that by now the regional centers will send out their heavy equipment to remove fallen trees. I am unable to contact Miranda,

Steven, or Mandy. Do you think I can make it out of here for a little while?"

"The storm has died down. It passed over the island quickly. If the roads are passable, you can. Be careful," Dr. Brown advised.

"As you are here, I will have to give it a try. I am worried about Ophelia," Raynor said. He turned to leave and then turned around again and said to Dr. Brown, "Can you tell Janet that I am going to check on Ophelia. She was worried about her."

"Sure, I will," he replied.

ASHES DISAPPEAR

Raynor managed to get to his car without much problem and drove off. There were fallen trees on parts of the roadway, as Dr. Brown said. There was no heavy equipment in sight and no hooded stranger. He got out of his car and attempted to move aside a fallen tree. He could not budge it. Someone suddenly appeared behind him and said, "Do you want to break your back, doc? Let me help you." It was the hooded stranger. He lifted the tree with one hand and shoved it aside. He did the same with a few others while Raynor stood watching him in amazement. Raynor was almost speechless as the man walked away. "Thank you. Can I offer you a lift somewhere?" Raynor asked, with his hand outstretched. The man disappeared before he could finish the sentence.

Raynor was puzzled and thought, "From where did he come? A Good Samaritan with the strength of Hercules, or did I just see a ghost?" He continued on his way and arrived at his home to see Miranda frozen at

the kitchen counter. He immediately located and restarted the power switch. Miranda resumed chopping the vegetables and did not seem to recall that she had ever stopped.
"Where is Ophelia?" he asked Miranda.
"She is at Steven and Mandy. I took her there this morning," she replied. Raynor ran out of his house across to Steven's house. He rang the doorbell, and Steven opened the door. "Are you and Mandy all right? How is Ophelia?" he asked.
"We are fine, and Ophelia is sound asleep. The horrid weather and the blackout scared her, but she settled down and fell asleep. Come inside," Steven beckoned to Raynor. Raynor sat down and told Steven about the strange man who moved the massive trees off the road and then disappeared. He also mentioned to him about Dr. Brown's encounter with that same man. Steven suddenly remembered that the urn with Zeeka's ashes had fallen and the ashes were scattered in the study.
He related to Raynor how it fell and broke after high winds blew the curtain over it. They both went into the study to check but

could find no trace of the ashes or pieces of the broken urn.
“Maybe Mandy cleaned it up,” Steven said. He called out to Mandy to ask her if she had cleaned up the ashes, and she stated that she had not and had forgotten about it.
“That is very strange,” said Steven.“The place looks as if it has been swept clean. Even the broken pieces of the urn are not there.”
Both Steven and Raynor searched under every item of furniture and found no trace of ashes or the urn. Mandy also searched and could not find any evidence of the broken urn or ashes.
“Should we tell anyone else about this?” Steven asked Raynor.
“I see no point in doing so,” said Raynor. “No one would believe such a story.”
“You are right,” said Steven, rubbing his eyes
Raynor took up his sleeping daughter from the next room, and before leaving, said to Steven, “I’ll call you later.”
Steven was puzzled. He sat down in the study and pondered over the matter. Where had the ashes gone? Even the broken

pieces of the urn were missing. He called out to Mandy again. “Mandy, are you sure you did not clean up the ashes?”
Mandy responded, “No, Steven. It was too dark to do any cleaning.” She walked into the room, sat down next to him, and said, “Steven, I cannot understand this. I am puzzled.”
“There must be some explanation for this,” Steven said. Suddenly, he recalled that when he went into the study during the power cut and reached for Ophelia’s baby bag, he felt as if someone had handed it to him. He dismissed that from his mind quickly, as he did not want to frighten Mandy by telling her that.

STEVEN SEES APPARITION

That night, Steven could not sleep. He tossed and turned on his bed, thinking about the disappearance of Zeeka's ashes. He was also thinking about how Zeeka had kidnapped him when he was just seven years old, and his brother Raynor was just two. He was still angry with Zeeka for taking him away from his parents, whom he loved with all his heart. After Zeeka had kidnapped him, a life with his parents and only brother had ended. His parents died, and he never saw them again.

It was almost midnight, and he was still awake. Just as he was about to doze off, he saw a white cloud hovering over his bed. *Was it smoke?* He opened his eyes wide. Whatever it was, it took shape, turned into the form of a man, and stood there looking at him. He rubbed his eyes and wondered if he was dreaming. His stomach tightened in knots. He could feel his face break out in a sweat. His heart was pounding so hard he thought that it would leap out of his chest. He held on tightly to Mandy, who was sound

asleep. She cried out in pain and woke up. "Steven, you are hurting me!"
The apparition disappeared. Steven was trembling. "What's the matter, love?" Mandy asked. Why are you still awake?"
"I saw something," he said.
"What is it?" she asked and turned on the light.
"I'm not sure. It was a nightmare," he replied. "I have an eerie feeling, though. I was careless with Zeeka's ashes. I should have disposed of those before we moved into this house."
"You're right, Steven. I wanted to suggest it, but it always slipped my mind. I never actually heard all the gory details about Zeeka from you. I saw the news reports. Raynor and Janet told me some of it, but you never spoke about it to me. Do you want to talk about it? How did he kidnap you?
"I was riding my bike home after visiting a friend who lived in a secluded part of the city. My bike broke down, and I was trying to fix it. A police jeep stopped, and the police officer asked if he could help. There was no one else in the vehicle.

I saw no harm in allowing a police officer to help since they are there to protect and serve. Or, so I thought. He came out of the vehicle, looked at my bike, turned it over, and tried to repair it. After a while, he said he could not fix it, and it needed to go to a bicycle shop. He offered to drive me home. I foolishly agreed, and I never saw my home again. What else do you know?" Steven asked Mandy.

"I know that you were only seven when he kidnapped you. You took a lift from him, as you trusted him. He was a police officer. You stayed with him all those years because he threatened to kill Raynor and your parents. I saw the flash drive that you had sent for Raynor in which you told him about your life with Zeeka. You talked about the zombies in that message. Do you think that Zeeka had something to do with your parents' death?"

"You know a lot, Mandy. Raynor and I have not discussed our parents' deaths. Maybe Zeeka was responsible," he said.

"I know that the police could not catch him, but Miranda the robot trapped him when he turned up at Raynor's house with a gun in

his hand asking for you. Miranda was home alone at the time. She did not know him, but when she saw the gun in his hand, she sensed that he was not a friend. She used her taekwondo skills to impair him, tied him, and activated her built-in security system to contact the police. She is wonderful. Maybe we should get a robot too," she said.
'One day we will," said Steven, whose thoughts were on the ghost he saw.
"You told me you had a nightmare. What was it about?" Mandy asked.
"I believe that I saw Zeeka's ghost," he replied.
Mandy's jaw dropped for a while.
"You mean you dreamt about Zeeka. Do you think that Zeeka rose up from the ashes and is haunting you?" She snuggled up to Steven as she said that. Steven hugged her and tried to reassure her that he was only dreaming. However, he knew that it was not a dream. He thought *that was Zeeka's ghost, and it was real*.
"Steven, my parents used to say that when someone commits suicide he cannot rest until the appointed time to die. Zeeka shot himself. He could be around for a long

period as a ghost. That is terrifying to think about," she said.
"You are right. Tomorrow we have to find the ashes and dispose of them. Let's try to get some rest now." He yawned as he spoke.

ZEEKA'S GHOST APPEARS

Next day Steven got up early and went into the study. He searched the entire area and could not find the ashes or broken pieces of the urn. He looked in the garden and then searched the entire house but found nothing. Mandy was dressed for work at the hospital, and he was not yet dressed. She called out to him, "Honey, hurry. We'll be late if we do not leave here in twenty minutes."

He gulped down a cup of coffee and ran upstairs to get dressed, but could not get his mind off the ghost he had seen the night before. They were both quiet as they drove to the hospital. Neither one brought up the subject about the ghost.

They arrived at the hospital and went their separate ways to their jobs.

Steven entered his office and sat down. His staff was already at their desks. Together with his team, he had formulated a procedure to eliminate Alzheimer's disease, and it was one of his greatest

achievements. An envelope was on his desk. He picked it up and opened it.
It was an invitation to attend a ceremony to honour him at the Gosh Hilton Hotel on a later date.
His staff was looking at him as he opened it and were observing his expression. He seemed distant and showed little emotion.
Dr. George Brown and some other doctors walked in and started clapping. He looked up, stood up, and smiled. They came towards him to hug him and congratulate him.
Dr. Brown said, "Steven you have brought fame to this small island of Gosh. You have achieved what no other scientist in any part of the world could do. Congratulations! We are indeed proud to have you on the staff of this hospital."
Raynor hugged him and said, "I am so proud of you brother."
Janet and Mandy also joined in the congratulations. Mandy said, "I knew I married the best scientist in the world. I am proud of my husband."
Mark Schmidt was present to offer congratulations and said, "This calls for a

celebration. Everyone is invited to the cafeteria for a special meal during the break." There was more clapping after that announcement.

In the evening Steven sat in his front porch and reflected on his life. He was a successful scientist despite the hardships he had undergone in his life. He knew he could never regain the lost life with his parents and brother. He missed his parents dearly and wished if they were there to celebrate his successes with him. He loved Mandy with all his heart and felt that he could not have wanted a better and supportive wife.

Mandy was downstairs in the kitchen preparing dinner. He could smell the delicious aroma of the food she was cooking. The smell of the food awakened his taste buds.

The sun hid behind a cloud, the sky darkened, the gentle breeze blew, and he fell asleep. He dreamt that he saw his biological father. He tried to reach for him to hug him, but his father kept his distance and said, "Son, I know what you have endured. I

am very proud of you. I am watching over you and Mandy."
After saying that he disappeared, and Steven awoke to hear Mandy calling out to him, "Steven honey, dinner is ready."
Steven ran downstairs and sat at the dinner table. Mandy had placed the delectable dishes on the table. Without waiting for her to start, he served himself and started eating. She sensed that something was wrong, as he seemed distracted. However, she decided to let him be. She knew that he needed time to think, and she allowed him to do so without disturbing him. After he had finished his dinner, he kissed her on her cheek and went into the study.
He tried turning on the light, but it would not go on. There was a hissing noise, and in the darkness, a cloud of smoke emerged in front of him and turned into the shape of a man who was barely visible. "Who are you? What do you want?" Steven asked in a trembling voice.
"I'm not here to harm you, Steven. I am your Dad," the ghost replied.
"Dad, Is that you? I thought it was Zeeka," Steven chirped.

“So what if I am Zeeka? I am still your Dad. I brought you up, Steven. I loved you. I still do,” Zeeka’s ghost replied.

“I do not want to hear about your dysfunctional love. Why are you here?” Steven asked.

“You are the reason I am here. You never committed my ashes to the ground. I cannot rest, and I cannot leave this place,” came the reply.

“But your ashes disappeared, and even the broken pieces of the urn are gone. What am I to do now?” Steven asked.

“Call the priest. He will know what to do,” was the reply.

At that moment, the doorbell rang, and Zeeka’s ghost disappeared.

Steven was all shaken up. He was angry and frustrated by the visits from Zeeka and was thankful that their meeting was interrupted.

Mandy called out, “Honey, we have guests. Janet, Raynor, and Ophelia are here.”

STEVEN TELLS RAYNOR

Steven was happy to see his brother, sister-in-law, and niece. He wanted to discuss the visits of Zeeka's ghost with Raynor.
After they had settled down and Mandy served tea and sandwiches, which they relished, Steven told Raynor about the visits from the ghost. He asked him not to mention it to Mandy or Janet, as he did not want to worry them.
Raynor was stunned to hear about Zeeka's ghost. His reaction was, "I never believed in ghosts. I thought that they only existed in stories. However, if you saw him and he spoke to you, then you must do as he says. Call the priest and let him do what he has to do."
"You are right. I will call the priest right away."
After Raynor and his family had left, Steven called his priest's office. The church secretary answered and said he was conducting a funeral service. She promised to advise the priest when he got back.

It was time to close up for the day, so she hurriedly wrote a note for the priest and placed it on his desk. As she turned her back, a gentle breeze blew the note underneath the desk. When the priest returned to his office, he saw no messages, and he packed up and went home.

As Steven lay in bed that night, he tried to recall his last meeting with Zeeka before his death.

He had reluctantly agreed to see Zeeka after Chief of Police Bernard Stern assured him that he would personally see to it that the prison officers protected him. When he went to see him, the officers brought Zeeka to the front to meet him. They chained him heavily to a chair and stood guard.

He asked, "What do you want to see me about? Have you not done enough harm in my life? Why did you come to Raynor's house yesterday and scare Miranda with a gun? Did you want to kill me?"

Grady replied, "No Steven, I did not want to kill you. I only wanted to apologize to you and to tell you why I kidnapped you forty years ago.

Steven was furious and shouted; "You are forty years too late. What can you say to me now that I do not know already?"
Zeeka went on, "Steven, I thought you were my son."
"Ha! What on earth made you think that?" asked Steven.
"Your mother and I were engaged to be married," Zeeka said.
Steven got up to leave and said, "I do not believe that. You are trying to manipulate me once again."
"Steven, please sit down. I am speaking the truth. Your mother and I were in love. We got engaged without her father's permission, and he did everything in his power to prevent our marriage."
Steven sat down, and Zeeka continued.
"The good doctor did not want his daughter to marry a police officer. He wanted her to marry your father, who was also a physician. She listened to her father, and she jilted me. I could not get over her. I thought that you were my son. I asked her, and she denied it. I did not believe her."
"You are a sick man. You thought I was your son, so you kidnapped me?" said Steven.

"I've loved you as if you were my own. I sent you to medical school so you'd become famous just as your biological father. Everything I have belongs to you.
I made a will. My attorney will contact you after I'm gone," said Zeeka.
"I do not want anything that belongs to you. After you are gone, you say. You're not going anywhere except behind bars for the rest of your life. You robbed me of my life with my parents and only brother. You forced me to create those zombies, which you told me you wanted to introduce into the police force as robots, instead of tracker dogs. However, what did you do? You used them to kill and maim people for your personal vendetta. I cannot listen to any more of this," said Steven, who got up to leave once more.
"Steven, I beg of you. Before you leave, please forgive me. I need your forgiveness. Please, Steven, forgive me," Zeeka pleaded.
Steven signaled to the officers to open for him, and without replying to Zeeka, he walked out.
The two officers returned Zeeka to his cell.

Later that night Zeeka committed suicide. Steven wondered if Zeeka wanted to hear him say that he forgave him. Maybe that was it. *Maybe if he told him that he forgave him, he would leave him alone.*

GHOST WARNS STEVEN

When Steven went downstairs in the morning, Mandy had already laid out a sumptuous breakfast. She greeted him with a kiss and said, "Darling, do you remember what day it is?"

Steven was still sleepy, as he did not get much sleep that night. He yawned, sat down, and said, "It is Saturday. Isn't it?" He raised the cup to his lips to sip his tea.

Mandy smiled broadly and said, "What are your plans for tonight, darling?"

Steven kept on yawning and said, "I cannot think of anything. Do you want to go somewhere special?"

Mandy laughed. "Steven darling, I cannot believe that you forgot about the event tonight.

You are being honored for inventing the cure for Alzheimer's disease."

She passed the newspapers to him and showed him the headlines. "Is it in the news, Mandy? Oh, honey, I have so much on my mind. I forgot all about it. Do you have an elegant dress to wear?"

"Of course I do. It is a surprise. I sent your suit to the dry cleaners. I will pick it up on my way home from the hairdresser."
"You think of everything darling. What will I do without you?" He leaned over and kissed her on her cheek.
Later in the day, Steven went into the study to write his speech for the night's event. Mandy had left to do some errands.
As he was making the final changes to the speech, he heard the ghostly sound.
The room turned to darkness, there was a hissing noise, and a cloud of smoke appeared in front of him. As the smoke dissipated, a figure emerged. It was Zeeka.
"You again!" Steven shouted.
"Steven, I am here to warn you."
"Warn me about what? Are you threatening me?" Steven said in an angry tone.
"No, I am not threatening you. Three men are planning to kill you."
Steven laughed loudly. "You come up with such ridiculous stories. You told me that you and my mother were engaged to be married, and you thought I was your child. For that reason, you kidnapped me and robbed me of life with my birth parents.

Why are you haunting me? Why don't you go to Hell or wherever you are destined for?"
"I am not joking. I heard these men talking in a bar outside of town. They are not satisfied with the money you gave them as compensation for the death of their loved ones. The zombies killed their relatives. They are planning to ambush and kill you."
"Ha! Ha! You were the cause of the death of those unfortunate people. I paid all the victims' families with the proceeds I received from your estate. I did not keep a cent for myself. Why would they want to kill me? The person responsible for the carnage was you, and you are already dead. Go away and leave me alone."
"Steven, I will go now. However, I cannot leave this world until the priest does his rituals. Did you call him?"
"Yes, I certainly did. He was not in, but his secretary promised to inform him that I called. I am still waiting for him to return my call."
"Very well. Be careful when you go out tonight."

“How did you know that I’m going out tonight?”
“There’s talk all over the island. You are being honoured for inventing a cure for Alzheimer’s disease.”
Zeeka’s ghost then disappeared with a hiss, leaving Steven puzzled.
Steven wondered, he seems to know everything taking place on the island. Being a ghost must be nice.

STEVEN IS HONOURED

Later that evening, the door opened, and Mandy walked in cheerfully with Steven's suit.

"Honey, I picked this up at the dry cleaners for you."

"Thank you, love," he replied and bent to kiss her cheeks.

Mandy looked at him and said, "Is something the matter, baby? You look like you've seen a ghost."

Steven shook his head. "It's nothing, darling. Is it time to get dressed for the big event?"

Mandy glanced at her watch and said, "We've only one hour, dear."

Taking her hand, Steven said, "All right. Let's get dressed, my love."

As they walked up the staircase to their bedroom together, Steven pondered. Should I tell Mandy what Zeeka's ghost said to me? No, I cannot do that. She will become paranoid.

One hour later, they walked down the staircase hand in hand.

Mandy looked gorgeous in an electric blue floor-length gown with spaghetti straps. The dress was ruched at the waist and form-fitting at the hips. The skirt flowed gently from her thighs. She wore her long, dark brown hair in a neat bun set in place with a diamond-studded hairpin. The colour of her dress and her dangling diamond earrings enhanced her blue eyes. She was the picture of elegance.

Steven was handsome in his five-piece black tuxedo suit, complete with jacket, white shirt, cummerbund, and bow tie. They made a dashing couple.

When they entered the exquisitely decorated ballroom of the Gosh Hilton Hotel, everyone stood up and clapped. Dr. Brown greeted them and led them to the head table. On the way to the head table, many colleagues held and kissed them. Amongst the specially invited guests were Chief of Police Bernard Stern, Dr. Raynor Sharpe, Dr. Janet Jones–Sharpe, Miranda the robot, Dr. George Brown, Dr. Mark Schmidt, Detective Jack Wildy, Detective Jerry Cole, Deputy Chief George Hammer,

Officer Cameron, Giselle Swan, and Attorney Tom Saunders.

Dr. Brown was the Master of Ceremonies. In his opening speech, he acknowledged the presence of all and continued:

"Ladies and gentlemen, as we all know, Alzheimer's disease is a neurological disorder in which the death of brain cells causes memory loss and cognitive decline. It is a neurodegenerative type of dementia, where the disease starts mild and gets progressively worse.

Many of us here have lost loved ones to this killer disease. While it may be too late to do anything for them, our renowned scientist, Dr. Steven Sharpe, has discovered a cure.

The product has been tested on many individuals, and it is proven to work. In fact, it is a miracle cure and a few people sitting in this audience will give their testimony here tonight. I now hand you over to the man of the moment, Dr. Steven Sharpe, whom we are proud to have as our Head of Research at the Gosh Hospital. He will give you all the details of this miracle drug."

There were loud cheers for Steven as he took to the podium.

After he had explained about the long hours of research, which led to the final discovery of the ingredients for the drug by his team of scientists, there were louder cheers and a standing ovation.
Several other persons made impromptu speeches to congratulate Steven and his team preceding the informal part of the event.
The dinner was sumptuous, and after dinner, there was dancing to the strains of the best band on the island.
All the guests had fun. Steven and Mandy were the centers of attention, and they were enjoying it when someone addressed Steven. “Dr. Steven Sharpe, we are very proud of you.”
Steven turned around to face Chief of Police Bernard Stern and said to him, “Thank you very much. I love my work at the hospital.”
“I can see that,” Stern replied. “Are you working on any more cures?”
“My team and I are always working on something, but I would not discuss it until we are very sure that we can alienate the disease.”

"Smart guy," replied Stern as he gave Steven a high five.
Jack Wildy and Jerry Cole did not miss the opportunity to throw some wisecracks at Steven.
Jack walked up to Steven and whispered, "Have you seen any zombies lately?"
Steven laughed and replied, "Have you checked the bushes?"
Jerry Cole remarked, "People usually say things like 'Long live Steven,' and I mean that Steven.
I want to add 'Stay dead Zeeka.' I could not handle another Zeeka on this island." They all laughed heartily on hearing that.
George Hammer and Officer Cameron walked up to Steven on overhearing the conversation. Hammer was amused and said, "We still have the Shrinkenator and demolisher 549 in case any zombies are spotted on the island." There was another burst of laughter.
Cameron chirped in, "Of course, and we still have Miranda the robot, with her taekwondo skills."

Although Steven was having fun, he began to feel uncomfortable on hearing talk of Zeeka and the zombies.
He had Zeeka's ghost to deal with, and he did not find these officers' jokes helpful.
He excused himself and walked over to Mandy, Janet, and Raynor.

STEVEN IS INTERVIEWED

"There you are, Steven," Raynor called out. "Janet and I are about to leave. Ophelia is with Janet's mom. We have to take her home."

"You're leaving already?" Steven asked.

"Yes, it is a good time for us to leave. Some reporters are here to interview you. We can take Mandy home if you like."

"That is a good idea. Take her home safely." A few thoughts ran through Steven's mind as he said that. At least Mandy would be safe at home. If anyone wants to harm me as Zeeka said, I will be alone. They cannot hurt Mandy. I will put up a brave fight knowing that Mandy is safe at home.

"Honey, are you all right? You seem distracted," said Mandy.

"No, sweetheart. It has been a long night. Let Janet and Raynor take you home. I will be a while here." He kissed her as he said that.

He turned to the reporters as Mandy, Janet, and Raynor left. Mandy looked around at Steven and said, "I love you." Steven blew her a kiss.

"Let's get on with this interview," he told reporters. The female reporter named Aggie posed the questions to Steven.
"Dr. Sharpe, we have a transcript of your speech which you made earlier today. I have all the information about how you and your team created the cure for Alzheimer's disease. However, I need some information about your background. Tell us about your childhood."
Steven replied, "I believe that everyone on this island knows about my childhood. It has been on every newspaper over the last two years. What specifically don't you know?"
Aggie answered, "Dr. Sharpe, you are right. It is a routine question, but if you do not want to go down that road again, I will omit that from the interview.
"No," Steven said. "I want you to mention that I am the son of Dr. Carl Sharpe and Mrs. Margaret Sharpe. Zeeka kidnapped me when I was seven years old and robbed me of a life I can never recover. He changed my name to Jason Stephens. He is dead and gone, and I am glad to be free of him. I will continue to do my best in the field of medicine to help my fellow citizens."

“Dr. Sharpe, what motivated you to study medicine?”
“I come from a family of doctors. My father was one, my mother was a nurse, and my only brother is a doctor. I guess it is in the blood.” Steven replied.
Aggie continued, “Dr. Sharpe, did Zeeka pay your tuition fees?”
Steven was getting agitated, but he tried to remain calm. “Yes, he did. He called me his son.”
“Did you call him Dad?” Aggie asked nervously.
“No. I begged him to send me back to my parents, but he refused.”
“While you were studying abroad, did you have an opportunity to escape from him?”
“He was a rogue police officer, and he had his henchmen watching me all the time. He threatened me on several occasions that if I ever tried to escape, he would kill my parents and only brother.”
“Did your parents ever try to look for you?”
“I believe they did. My mother died one year after I disappeared. I was unaware of her death at the time. My father passed away

after my brother graduated from The Faculty of Medicine."

"Did you ever get close to Zeeka?"

"I never did. I hated Zeeka all my life and never want to see him again."

"He is dead, sir. You will never see him again."

Steven thought she did not know that his ghost was haunting him. How could she know?

Aggie pressed on. She knew that she was digging up old dirt but asked, "You never felt close to him. You hated him all your life. Why did you help him to create those zombies that created havoc in the lives of so many citizens?'

Steven struggled to be patient and replied, "I answered that question two years ago. I did not help him create zombies. He demanded that I create a vaccine to bring dead babies to life. I gave the serum to him and he injected the babies. I thought it was just an experiment. I was under duress. He kept threatening to kill my parents and brother if I did not obey him. The law has cleared me of any wrongdoing."

"I understand, Dr. Sharpe. I will let you go now. Thanks for the interview."

Steven thanked Dr. Brown and his colleagues for planning an enjoyable evening for him and prepared to leave. It seemed that no one else was in a hurry to go home. They were eating, drinking, and making merry. A sudden fear overtook him as he stepped into the darkness of the night. Although there were lights everywhere, the place looked gloomy.

He had parked his car in the multi-storey car park. It was lonely, and he feared if Zeeka's ghost would appear again. He recalled Zeeka's words. *I am not joking. I heard these men talking in a bar outside of town. They are not satisfied with the money you gave them as compensation for the death of their loved ones. The zombies killed their relatives. They are planning to ambush and kill you.*

He looked all around him as he stepped into the glass elevator. No one was in sight. He arrived on the ninth floor safely, got into his car, made the downward spiral out of the carpark and headed home. *Zeeka was*

wrong. No one wanted to kill him, he thought.
He drove into the car park of his home and drew a breath of relief. The event was great. Everyone enjoyed it. Just that nosy reporter wanted to dig up the past and stir up his emotions. Zeeka's ghost was not around. He and Mandy could have a peaceful night all to themselves. She looked beautiful and desirable tonight. He longed to hold her in his arms.
He turned his key in the lock on the front door, but it was already open. He walked into the hallway. Either Mandy had forgotten to close the door, or she left it open for him so he would not have to waste time opening it.
He ran up the staircase to the bedroom calling, "Mandy, honey, I am home."
Mandy did not answer. Maybe she was waiting on the bed to surprise him. "Ready or not, here I come," he crooned.
There was no sign of Mandy. He ran up and down the staircase searching the house, but there was no Mandy.

An idea struck him. She probably stayed at Raynor and Janet until I got home. I will call Raynor.
He called Raynor's home, and Janet answered. "Janet, is Mandy at your place?"
Janet was surprised at this question and asked, "Isn't she at home? We watched her enter the house."
"Is Mandy playing a joke on me? Tell her that I miss her. I want her home now."
"This is no joke. Is Mandy missing?" Janet asked in a solemn voice.
Steven's head started pounding. Could Zeeka be right? No, he was wrong. Mandy must be around somewhere.
"We are coming over now, Steven," Janet said. She sounded very concerned. Steven started panicking. He ran around the house looking for clues for what may have happened to Mandy. *No. No. This can't be right.*
Within seconds, Janet and Raynor arrived with concerned looks on their faces. "Are you sure she is not in the pool area?" Raynor asked.
"She will not be there so late at night," Steven responded as he paced the floor.

"I will go and check," said Janet in an anxious tone.

"Raynor," Steven called." I have something to say to you."

"What is it, Steven?" asked Raynor as he walked up close to him.

"Zeeka's ghost appeared to me a few more times. He told me that he overheard some men talking outside of town. They are not satisfied with the money I gave them as compensation for the death of their loved ones. The zombies killed their relatives. They are planning to ambush and kill me."

"Why are you only telling me this now?" Raynor asked.

"He only told me this today before we left home to attend the event," Steven replied.

"He must be speaking the truth. Those men are probably using Mandy as bait to get to you. We will have to get Detectives Jack Wildy and Jerry Cole involved. I will call Jack now," said Raynor.

Janet had just stepped back inside, and she overheard the conversation. "Is this true?" she asked. Steven nodded his head.

Janet broke down in tears and said in between sobs, "We must find my sister.

Yes, get hold of Detectives Jack Wildy and Jerry Cole."

JACK AND JERRY INTERVENE

Raynor made the call, and within minutes, Jack Wildy and Jerry Cole turned up on the doorstep.
"What's the problem, doc? Your wife's gone missing?" asked Jack.
Raynor was quick to answer. "Janet and I brought her home while Steven was being interviewed by reporters at the hotel. We saw her enter the house. When Steven returned home, she was not in the house."
"Did you all see any signs of a struggle?" Jack asked.
"No," Steven replied.
"Did she change her dress that she was wearing tonight? If I must say so, she looked fabulous in that electric blue dress. If she changed her clothes, it must be in the bedroom. Did you check?" Jack looked at Steven when he said that.
"I did not think about that. I will check now, "replied Steven.
All four went up to the bedroom and looked around. They checked the bathroom and cupboards. The dress was not there. Steven

said, "Even her shoes that she wore are not here."
Jerry Cole interjected, "That means she did not even go to the bedroom when she returned home. Nothing seems out of place. Is anything missing?" Steven shook his head. "It does not appear so."
Jerry Cole was in deep thought for a while. He looked up and asked Steven, "Are you telling us everything? Did you receive any threats lately? Did you receive any notes or calls for ransom money?"
"If I tell you everything you will not believe me," Steven said in a gruff voice.
"Try us," said Jack.
Steven ventured to relate to Jack and Jerry his meetings with Zeeka's ghost and what he told him about three men who were planning to hurt him.
Jack waited for quite a while before responding. "You talked to a ghost? You believe it was Zeeka's ghost?"
Steven replied, "Yes, we spoke about other stuff. I know it was Zeeka."
"So you are saying that we should listen to the ghost of a man who killed a multitude of people when he was alive. Can this evil

entity lead us to your wife?" Jack asked in a sarcastic tone.
Jerry got up and walked towards the front door. He bent and picked up something from behind a plant. He returned with the object. It sparkled as he dangled it in the air and said to Steven, "Is this your wife's earring?"
Steven jumped up. "Yes, she wore a pair of diamond earrings to the function. That is one side."
"There appear to be scuff marks from several pairs of shoes at the entrance. Maybe your wife was grabbed as she entered the house. Raynor and Janet, did you see any strange vehicles parked close by when you dropped off Mandy?"
Janet looked out the window and said, "Yes, there was a large black van, a Mercedes, parked on the street but not directly in front of the house. It is no longer there."
"Do you recall the license plate and number?" Jack inquired.
"No. I looked at it as we drove off. Um, Maracas24--," Janet said quickly. "I do not recall the entire number. I am sorry."

“My God. Are you saying that my wife was kidnapped?” said Stephen.
“Looks that way,” said Jack. “Jerry, call the station. Tell Marge to track the owners of any black Mercedes van with license plate Maracas and number beginning with 24. Doc, if you have not yet received a call for ransom for your wife, it means that they want you to come and get her.
Zeeka’s ghost may be right. They are after you. I am confident that you will receive a phone call soon. We will have to devise a plan. At the police station, we will set up equipment to monitor all your calls. We have a fast-track tracing method. Once a call is made to your home or cell phone, we will have the call traced within seconds. We can even capture photos of the callers. There would be no escape for them. Do not worry. Your wife will return to you.”

MANDY WAS KIDNAPPED

Mandy slowly opened her eyes and looked around. She was lying in a van, all bound and tied up. Her hands and feet were tied with plastic straps, and there was duct tape over her mouth. She was unable to move, and she felt suffocated. She was in a daze and felt as if she were drugged.

She was in a mess. Her diamond-studded pin was removed from her hair, and her dark brown hair was loose about her shoulders.

The van swerved into a lonely track and pulled up next to a secluded house on the beach. Rough hands grabbed her and removed the duct tape from her mouth with such force that she screamed out in pain.

“Shut up!” shouted a masked man.

“Leave me alone,” she shouted back, as two masked men pulled her out of the van and dragged her into the house.

“Sit there and be quiet. I’ve a phone call to make,” said the burly-looking one with the mask.

Mandy tried to get a good look at the men, but the masks on their faces prevented her from seeing them. "What do you want with me?" she asked.

"If your husband cares about you, he'll come looking for you. We want him," the shorter one responded.

"What did he do to you?" she asked.

"You'll know soon enough. Sit there and don't cause any trouble or we will kill you." The burly one glared at her as he said that. He pulled out his cell phone and called Steven's home phone number. No one answered the phone.

"Where's your husband? You left home for a couple of hours, and he already forgot you. Does that man care about you?" He jeered at her. "Do you have his cell number?

Mandy replied, "Is it money you want?"

"I asked for his cell number, woman. Worry about your life. Give me the phone number," he shouted.

The other kidnapper said to him, "Go easy on her Matt. She's not responsible for what happened two years ago."

"Fool, you called my name in front of her. Now I'll have to get rid of both of you," Matt blurted out.

“Calm down, pal. There are many guys called Matt. She has not seen our faces. I’m on your side,” said the short one.
“I will give you the number. It is 777- 6366,” said Mandy, who was in tears. Matt dialed the number, and Steven answered. He turned on the speaker so that Raynor and Janet could hear the conversation.
“Dr. Steven Sharpe, if you want to see your wife alive, get here within five hours with three million dollars. I’ll tell you where to bring it, but you must come alone.”
“I cannot raise that kind of money in five hours, especially at this time of night. Where’s my wife? I want to talk to her.” Steven demanded.
“Let me talk to him please,” Mandy pleaded with tears streaming down her face.
“I know that you have money in your safe at home. Bring the money, and you will get your wife,” Matt said to Steven.
Steven knew he did not have money in his safe, and that it was impossible to get that amount of money in the short time frame stipulated, but he said to him,
“Wait, do not hang up. Give me the directions to get there. I’ll bring the money.”

It was Steven's intentions to keep the kidnapper talking so that Detectives Jack Wildy and Jerry Cole could trace the call.

"Drive twenty miles to South Beach, turn left at the turnpike, drive one more mile, and turn left into the first track leading to the beach.

You will see a black van parked outside the house, "Matt replied.

"I'll be there as soon as I can, with the money. Mandy, I love you." Steven hoped that Mandy would hear his voice.

STEVEN IS IN DANGER

As soon as Steven turned off his phone, Jerry Cole called. "We traced that call, doc. We're on our way to the kidnappers' place with plenty of back up. I would advise you to stay at home. You should not walk into the path of those killers."
"No, I'm going. I want to make sure that I bring Mandy home safely," replied Steven.
Jerry was emphatic, "Steven, we are firmly advising against it. Allow the police to do their work."
Steven turned off the phone, ran out of the house, and was followed by Raynor who called out to him, "Steven, how are you going to deal with this? You cannot go there without the money. I'm going with you. Wait for me."
Steven shouted, "You stay home brother. Your wife and daughter need you. I'm going alone." His car screeched as he swung out of the driveway and sped down the road leaving Raynor stunned.
Steven's head was reeling. He could not imagine what Mandy was going through with

those evil men. *Mandy needs me*, he thought. *I'm coming to get you, sweetheart, even if it costs me my life.* There was a hissing sound, and Zeeka's ghost appeared and sat in the passenger seat next to him.
"What are you doing here?" asked Steven.
"I'm going with you. I will help you through this. I'm responsible for this, and I'll put an end to it," Zeeka's ghost replied.
"Your overzealous affection for me has already cost me a life with my real family. Why do you keep hounding me, even after you're dead?"
"Steven, I love you. I'm not going to allow anyone to hurt you."
"Well, then hang on, as you're going to get the ride of your life. My aim is to rescue my wife."
"I cannot die twice. However, if you want to save Mandy be careful how you drive."
"Can anyone else see you in my car?"
Steven glanced in the rearview mirror to see if the people in the car behind saw a ghost in his vehicle.
"Only you can see me."
"So how are you going to help me?"
"Do you have any weapon, Steven?"

“No,” Steven replied emphatically.
“So how do you intend to defend Mandy and yourself?”
“Detectives Jack Wildy and Jerry Cole are on their way with a backup team.”
“At the speed you are driving, you will get there before they do. What is your plan?”
“Truthfully, I have none,” Steven said, as he glanced over at Zeeka’s ghost. He was amazed that he was not even scared of him.
“Those men are killers, Steven. They’re not going to release Mandy because you demand they do so. You should wait until the police arrive.”
Steven drove into the track and sped up to the house and parked a fair distance away. He jumped out of the car. There was no sign of Zeeka’s ghost. “Have you abandoned me after all your talk that you are here to help me?”
There was no answer from Zeeka’s ghost, and Steven could not see him.

GHOST STOPS KIDNAPPERS

Steven sneaked up to the side of the house and peeked through a window. He saw Mandy sitting there, bound and gagged and looking disheveled. He became enraged. He brazenly knocked on the door. Matt came out. "Look who the cat dragged in," he said. "You have walked into our trap."

Matt held Steven by the shirt collar and pulled him into the room saying, "Say goodbye to your wife now." Mandy tried to speak but could not. She shook her head violently as if to tell the attackers not to hurt her husband.

Steven shouted, "Do you want your money? It's in the car outside."

Matt's face lighted up. " Did you bring the three million?"

Steven replied, "You want to count it? Send your friend for it." He held up his car keys.

Matt turned to his short friend and said, "Grant, take his car keys and go get the cash."

Grant took the keys and before leaving the room, he asked Steven, "Where did you park your car?"

"Not too far from the house," Steven replied.

Matt kept glancing out the window to keep an eye on Grant.

There was a hissing sound in the room. Steven knew it was Zeeka. Matt looked around bewildered. He saw no one. Before he realized what had happened, he fell to the floor, and his gun flew out of his hand.

"Who is that? I cannot see anybody," he shouted.

Steven grabbed the gun while a confused Matt tried to figure out how Steven did that to him.

Steven pointed the gun menacingly at Matt and said, "Untie my wife now, or you are dead."

Matt obeyed, and Mandy was free within seconds. Mandy ran to Steven and stood at his side being careful not to disturb his focus. Grant walked in, and his jaw dropped when he saw Steven holding the gun.

"Where's the money?" Matt asked Grant.

"There was nothing in the car," he replied.

"You are a double-crosser. I'll kill you and your wife," Matt shouted at Steven.
"I'm holding the gun," Steven said in a commanding voice. "Grant, tie your friend up. The police will be here shortly."
Grant tied up Matt while Steven pointed the gun in their direction. Grant was trembling. He mumbled to Matt, "I should never have listened to you. We'll both end up in prison."
Sounds of police sirens filled the air. Detectives Jack Wildy and Jerry Cole walked in with their team. Both Matt and Grant were arrested and taken away in a police vehicle.
"Sorry, we could not get here earlier. Raynor called and told us that you came here alone. You're a brave man, Steven," Jack said. Turning to Mandy, he said, "Your husband is a hero. You're a lucky woman."
He turned again to Steven and whispered, "Your ghost was right."
Steven and Mandy hugged, kissed, and expressed their undying love for each other. On their way home, Steven wondered if he should tell Mandy that Zeeka's ghost was real. He decided against it.

STEVEN FORGIVES ZEEKA

When Steven and Mandy arrived home, Janet and Raynor dropped in to discuss the harrowing events of the past few hours. They left quite late.

Mandy went to the bedroom to take a hot bath, and Steven went into the study and sat down.

He was secretly hoping that Zeeka's ghost would appear and he would thank him for all he did for Mandy and him. His wish came true. Zeeka's ghost appeared.

Steven was excited to see him, and the first words that came out of his mouth were, "I forgive you. I know that you came to help me."

Zeeka's ghost replied, "Thank you, Steven. Your forgiveness means everything. I can now go in peace to the other side."

Steven said, "Was it you who moved the fallen trees that were blocking the road after the storm? Both Raynor and Dr. Brown stated that a stranger lifted the trees and put them aside to allow their cars to pass."

Zeeka replied, "Yes, Steven. I moved the trees. I wanted to atone for my sins and to

seek your forgiveness. You have forgiven me, so my path is now clear."
Steven said, "But what about all the people that were killed because of those zombies you unleashed on them? Don't you need their forgiveness?"
"You helped the families of those people. Your actions helped my soul. You have now forgiven me, and that is the final act. You would not see me again. I love you, Steven."
As Zeeka's ghost started disappearing, Steven said, "Thanks for all your help. Thanks for saving Mandy and me from those hoodlums."
Zeeka replied, "You forgot that I was a police officer? Bye, Steven."
Steven wondered, why do I feel such a profound sense of sadness because I would no longer be seeing him?
The next morning, Steven received an unexplained call from the priest. The priest said that someone took an urn with ashes and told him that Steven wanted to have the ashes committed. He was prepared to do it that very afternoon if Steven agreed. Steven answered in the affirmative.

After the conversation with the priest, Steven felt that he had no choice but to tell Mandy the truth about Zeeka's ghost and the part the ghost played in saving them from the evil kidnappers. He also decided to surprise Mandy and grant her wish by investing in a robot just like Miranda.

THE END

ZEEKA CHRONICLES

What if paradise became a biotech battleground?

ZEEKA CHRONICLES: REVENGE OF ZEEKA has been adapted into a five-series screenplay for a movie or TV series.

This futuristic thriller was an award winner in the category, Young Adult Thriller in Reader's Favorite International Awards

2018, winner of the gold award in the category Science Fiction in Connections Emagazine Readers' Choice Awards 2018, and placed in the top ten finalists for science fiction in the Author Academy Global Awards 2018.

The book is a Caribbean Sci-Fi Thriller written by Brenda Mohammed, who has published 68 books and three screenplays.

The futuristic sci-fi thriller is set in the year 2036.

A fictitious tropical island off South America hides a sinister secret.

A rogue scientist's army of zombies and cyborgs causes carnival celebrations to erupt into chaos.

A brave detective must confront the horrors of artificial intelligence, revenge, and genetic manipulation.

Paradise turns perilous, but with human resilience, good triumphs over evil.

The storytelling by Author Brenda Mohammed is cinematic.

The unique setting, Caribbean culture, and futuristic suspense will appeal to fans of Frankenstein, Twilight Zone, and Black Mirror.

The novel explores the dark possibilities of artificial intelligence, human ambition, and vengeance in a futuristic Caribbean. Perfect for fans of high-concept science fiction, biotech suspense, and readers seeking underrepresented voices in speculative fiction.

The story is purely the author's imagination, inspired by the zika virus in 2016. Zombies and robots take centre stage.

The mind-blowing story begins in Zeeka and the Zombies Episode 1 and continues in Zeeka's Child Episode 2, Zeeka Returns Episode 3, Zeeka's Ghost Episode 4, and Resurrection Episode 5. Books for each episode are also sold separately.

Reader's Favorite International gave Zeeka Chronicles a five-star review.

Here is an extract of that review:

"Zeeka Chronicles is a thoughtful series and would delight fans of the genre.

Brenda Mohammed is an author brimming with original ideas, and definitely an author to follow."

ZEEKA AND THE ZOMBIES II

ZEEKA AND THE ZOMBIES II, a gripping sci-fi horror novel, was adapted into a four-series screenplay and was selected as a finalist in the 13Horror-com Film & Screenplay Contest 2025.
The futuristic sci-fi horror thriller written by Trinidadian Brenda Mohammed, who has published 68 books to date, was selected among the top 25% of entries.

The feature-length screenplay based on this novel was praised by judges for its genre-defying fusion of futuristic sci-fi, Caribbean folklore, and dark fantasy, set in a vividly imagined 2036 Caribbean Island.
Andrew Hannon, the Contest Director and one of the Hollywood judges, commended the screenplay for its complex narrative, emotional depth, and cinematic horror, highlighting standout moments such as the Carnival massacre, the twist involving Chief of Police Bill Grady, and the poignant revelation of Zeeka's hidden humanity.
A psychotic cop, who has adopted the alias MASTER ZEEKA, unleashes a horde of zombies upon a Caribbean paradise amidst its carnival festivities. It’s up to two long-separated brothers, with a surprising connection to the cop, to save the day.
The sci-fi horror novel is loaded with several twisty thrills and intriguing revelations. The brothers Dr. Raynor Sharpe and Dr. Steven Sharpe, a malicious zombie horde, two detectives, and Master Zeeka, who created the zombies, are the main characters of the novel.

Number Nine, the zombie who discovered he was not a zombie, but just struggling with a strange illness, is cured by Dr. Steven Sharpe with a Miracle Machine he invented. Readers of Caribbean sci-fi horror and zombie fiction will love this story.

REVENGE OF ZEEKA HORROR TRILOGY

REVENGE OF ZEEKA: HORROR TRILOGY contains the first three books of the Zeeka Chronicles, a five-book series that has been adapted into a screenplay. Zeeks and the Zombies II, which contains four books in the series, has also been adapted into a screenplay and is a finalist in the horror-comedy Film & Screenplay Contest in September 2025.

Reviewed by Faridah Nassozi for Readers' Favorite

In Revenge of Zeeka by Brenda Mohammed, the island of Gosh is under attack by an army of zombies under the command of a vengeful science genius. In the year 2016, the Zika virus broke out in Central and South America with life-threatening effects on pregnant women. Given a choice to save the mothers or the unborn babies, a decision was made to save the mothers. The tiny stillborns were securely and secretly buried.

Only a few people knew of this. Unknown to everyone, however, a certain scientist managed to get hold of all 51 bodies, bring them back to life, and condition them to follow his command, creating himself a perfect army of zombies.

Now, twenty years later, the evil scientist seeks revenge on those he holds responsible for the stillbirths. Only three of the current doctors at Central Hospital - Raynor, Mark, and George - witnessed the unfortunate events of 2016. The three have strong suspicions about who might be controlling the zombies.

Meanwhile, Zeeka is lying in wait for the perfect time to unleash his army onto the island. Zeeka has big, evil plans and this is just the beginning. In a desperate search for answers, and with very little to go on, the doctors search for the elusive Master Zeeka. Will they save the islanders from Zeeka and his zombies, or will it be too late? Revenge of Zeeka by Brenda Mohammed is a one-of-a-kind novella trilogy that delivers an incredible story guaranteed to give readers an absolute sci-fi treat. I especially liked how Brenda used current events as the pivotal point from which to build this amazing sci-fi horror.

This made the story even more relatable. More importantly, however, I admired how she owned her story and created this captivating version of events.

She captured with amazing depth the setting, characters, plot, and emotions in so few words.

If you are looking for a thrilling short read, this fast-paced, sci-fi action novella will give you the time of your life

RESURRECTION

Resurrection: Revenge of Zeeka Book 5 is the grand finale in the mind-boggling five-book Science fiction series Revenge of Zeeka. Someone resurrected and it is not Zeeka.

Number Nine, the zombie, who police thought was dead in the massacre at the Carnival event in February 2036 is alive.
Mandy's robot helper, Eve, encounters a stranger in the backyard.
When Eve tells him she is a robot, he tells her his story. Eve promises to keep their discussion a secret but records the conversation on her security device and plays it for Steven and Mandy.
Number Nine collapses in the backyard with an epileptic fit, and Eve alerts the Gosh hospital. Tests and records confirm that he is Number Nine. He is not a zombie and is the biological son of Bill Grady – Master Zeeka, who made him grow up with zombies because he was misdiagnosed with microcephaly- a disease associated with the zika virus that infected his mother, Angelina Grady, who died in childbirth. His name is Nieman Grady and is 22 years old.
Steven faces opposition to the launch of his most significant invention of the century.
Nieman Grady - Number Nine is the first volunteer to test it and is healed of his neurological disorder.
Here is an extract from a review.

'While the series started with possible abuse of medical technology, the last book leaves us hopeful that technology can one day serve us better than most of us can imagine.'

AUTHOR BIOGRAPHY

OVERVIEW

Brenda Mohammed is a prolific, multi-award-winning author and screenwriter from Trinidad and Tobago, with 68 published books and 68 audiobooks spanning various genres, including science fiction, memoirs, mystery, romance, self-help, poetry, children's books, anthologies, magazines, and three screenplays. Her superb writing skills won her several International literary awards, bringing fame to Trinidad and Tobago in the field of Literature. Brenda Mohammed's literary catalogue is a testament to the power of words, creativity, and resilience.

INTERNATIONAL RECOGNITION

1. Biz Weekly published Brenda's work in September 2025.
2. Her literary journey was published in USA NEWS in September 2025.
3. The Ethiopian Herald published an interview with Brenda Mohammed in 2021.
4. Her work in Literature was featured in the local newspapers in Trinidad and Tobago on several occasions.

PREVIOUS OCCUPATIONS

a. Before her literary ascent, Brenda was a trailblazer in banking and insurance, rising from a clerk at the tender age of 16 to senior leadership at a local bank in Trinidad. Her career helped shape communities and drive economic growth across Trinidad and Tobago.

b. After she retired from Banking, she excelled in insurance, earning the prestigious Million Dollar Round Table qualification six times, and a Life Underwriting Fellowship from the American College, USA, and earning international recognition as a top-tier financial professional from Trinidad and Tobago.

LITERARY JOURNEY AND ACCOLADES

1. Her writing journey began after surviving a near-fatal battle with cancer. That experience birthed I AM CANCER FREE, a bestselling memoir that won global acclaim. The book won an award in the Reader's Favorite International Awards 2018.

2. Her gripping five-series futuristic Caribbean sci-fi thriller, ZEEKA CHRONICLES, won an award in the Reader's Favorite International Awards 2018, and has been adapted into a five-part screenplay, primed for film or television. The book also won awards in Science Fiction in SIBA Awards 2017, won the gold award in the category Science Fiction in Connections Emagazine Readers' Choice Awards 2018,

and was a winner in the top ten finalists for science fiction in the Author Academy Global Awards 2018.

3. Her four-series futuristic sci-fi horror screenplay, ZEEKA AND THE ZOMBIES II, is a finalist in a film and screenplay contest 2025, by 13Horror-com. This recognition marks a major milestone in Brenda's journey to bring her literary universe to the screen, reinforcing her reputation as a visionary storyteller with global impact

4. Her romance novel, THE GIFT OF LOVE, has also been adapted into a short screenplay for television and made it to the Quarterfinals of the Stage 32 Drama Box Screenwriting Competition in April 2026.

5. Her memoir, MY LIFE AS A BANKER, won second place for 'best memoir' in the Metamorph Publishing Summer Indie Book Awards 2016.

6. Her self-help guide, HOW TO WRITE FOR SUCCESS I, was hailed by the Ethiopian Herald as "a comprehensive toolkit for writers, critics, and editors." In August 2019, How to Write for Success I topped all the books in the Non-Fiction category of Connections Emagazine

Readers' Choice awards and won the gold medal in the category of non-fiction.
It also placed second in all categories and won the silver medal. It was a triple victory for Brenda, because her romance novel, 'Stories People Love,' placed first in all categories and won the gold medal.
7. BARRY HOLMES MYSTERIES received a five-star review from Readers' Favorite International in September 2021, won the Culture, Literature, and Research [CLR] Award in India for Best Writer- Fantasy, received a certificate of recognition from The International Chamber of Writers and Artists [CIESART], Spain in 2023 on World Book Day, and was a finalist in the Independent Author Awards 2024 hosted by Literary Global Awards.
8. STORIES PEOPLE LOVE topped the Connections Emagazine Readers' Choice Awards 2019, and won two gold medals in the category Romance and the other for topping all genres.
9. In 2025, CIESART GLOBAL honoured Brenda Mohammed with the UNION OF NATIONS SUCCESS AWARD and the MEDAL OF HONOUR for her outstanding

career, significant merits, and valuable contributions in the fields of humanities, culture, science, and intercultural dialogue. Her picture was chosen as the face on CIESART'S GLOBAL MAGAZINES twice between 2023 and 2026.

LITERARY APPOINTMENTS

1. She was appointed by the President of CIESART GLOBAL as National President for CIESART [Cámara Internacional de Escritores & Artistas] Trinidad and Tobago in 2022.
2. She founded the How to Write for Success Facebook Literary Forum in 2016 and has mentored countless writers, published anthologies, and magazines that uplift voices worldwide. She continues to champion literature as a force for good. Her leadership has provided a space where writers are not only creators but crusaders, using their craft to heal, educate, and inspire.
3. A Peace Ambassador for the Facebook group, LOGOS LITERATURE, and advocate against domestic and all types

of violence and suicide, Brenda's influence extends beyond the page.

4. She's a member of Stage 32, connecting her to the global film and TV community, and continues to inspire through humanitarian work, literary leadership, and cinematic storytelling.

In a world where stories shape lives, Brenda Mohammed emerges as a beacon, her words healing wounds, building communities, and transforming the literary landscape from Trinidad and Tobago to the world stage.

Her catalogue showcases not only her immense talent but also her deep commitment to addressing both personal and global challenges through storytelling. Below is a curated overview of her diverse and impactful body of work.

BOOKS BY AUTHOR

CHILDREN'S BOOKS: NURTURING YOUNG MINDS AND HEARTS.

Brenda's children's books introduce young readers to the world through heart-warming and imaginative stories that captivate the imagination while imparting valuable lessons.

Adventures of Squeaky Doo (2014) takes readers on the travel memoirs of a beloved teddy bear, sharing the wonder of discovery.

She Cried for Me (2017) offers a poignant autobiography from the perspective of a stray dog, combining empathy with an important message about compassion.

The Child Poet (2020) brings poetry to children, inviting them into a poetic galaxy full of wonder and creativity. This book became a hot release upon publication, delighting young minds with verse.

PSYCHOLOGICAL THRILLERS: UNRAVELLING MINDS AND MYSTERIES.

Brenda's psychological thrillers are gripping, fast-paced, and designed to keep readers on the edge of their seats. Her ability to weave suspense with character complexity makes her a standout in the genre.

The Manipulator (2021) delves deep into the mind of a manipulative figure, leaving readers questioning trust and human behaviour.

Conspiracy Stories (2021) features three chilling tales that awaken the mind and explore the dark side of human nature.

MYSTERY THRILLERS: TALES OF CRIME, SUSPENSE, AND ROMANCE

The Barry Holmes Series (2020), a mix of crime fiction and romance, is one of Brenda's most popular works, capturing the intrigue and mystery of disappearances and unsolved crimes. Three mysterious disappearances bring together three mind-bending mysteries that leave readers questioning the truth.

The Gift of Love (2018) mixes crime fiction with romance, engaging readers in a plot that keeps them guessing.

The Axe Murderer (2019) takes on kidnapping and suspense, blending shocking twists with emotional depth.

What Happened to Mary Loo (2020) explores the mystery of a post-lockdown disappearance.

.

MEMOIRS: SHARING STORIES OF LIFE AND RESILIENCE:

Brenda's memoirs offer an intimate look at her life and the experiences that have shaped her. These stories of resilience, family, and career offer inspiration and reflection.

I Am Cancer Free (2013) recounts her miraculous recovery from cancer, offering hope and strength to others facing illness.

Memoirs of Dr. A. M. Khan (2014) sheds light on her father's life during Indentureship in Trinidad and Tobago, revealing a deeply personal family history.

My Life as a Banker (2014) chronicles Brenda's journey through the banking sector, offering motivational insights into the world of business.

Retirement is Fun (2014) captures the adventures and joys of life after her banking career, showcasing her ability to find fulfilment in new chapters.

Travel Memoirs with Pictures (2014) presents a visual journey around the world, blending storytelling with the beauty of photography.

CHRISTIAN BOOKS OF FAITH, INSPIRATION, AND WISDOM

Blending poetic inspiration with biblical teachings, Brenda's Christian books speak to the heart, providing spiritual guidance and encouragement.

Titles like Your Time Is Now, He is the One, Chosen by the Creator, God Fearing Ones, and Serenity in End Times (2014–2024) offer uplifting messages and biblical wisdom to help readers navigate life's challenges.

True Power of Love and Now is the Time encourage faith-driven living, while Keys to Withstanding Storms of Life and Highway to Joy Eternal offer practical advice to find strength in times of hardship. Christmas Messages [2025] tells why Jesus is the reason for the season.

POETRY COLLECTIONS: REFLECTIONS OF THE SOUL.

Brenda's poetry collections have touched readers' hearts by addressing universal themes of love, resilience, and identity. Collections like Strength for the Disheartened, Dreams of the Heart, and A Road Travelled (2019–2024) explore emotions ranging from loss to joy.
Chaotic Times (2021) capture the complexities of life, while Just for You and Treasured Memories celebrate love and personal reflection.
Sweet Medley [2020], Tea Time Poetry [2021] Truth and Save God's Earth [2024] cover Climate Change, Environmental Issues, and Fun Times.
Soothing Poetry in English and Spanish [2020] covers several topics.

Beauty of poetry [2024] explores peace, love, motivation, and other emotions. Islands in the Sun [2022] consists of poems about the Caribbean Islands.

ROMANCE: HEARTFELT AND ENDEARING TALES

Brenda's romance novels capture the beauty and complexity of relationships with heart-warming and tender narratives. Stories People Love (2014) and Heart-Warming Tales (2014) explore themes of love, connection, and the magic of romance. Stories that Intrigue (2019) presents a unique love story between two writers, blending creativity and passion.

SCIENCE FICTION – REVENGE OF ZEEKA SERIES – A FUTURISTIC SAGA

Brenda's Zeeka Chronicles is a science fiction series that combines thrilling narratives with futuristic elements, such as zombies, robots, and human resilience, where good triumphs over evil.

Titles like Zeeka and the Zombies (2016), Zeeka's Child, Zeeka Returns, and Zeeka's Ghost (2017) create a post-apocalyptic world where survival and courage are paramount. Resurrection, Revenge of Zeeka Horror Trilogy, and the award-winning Zeeka Chronicles (2016–2017) complete the saga, which was also adapted into a five-part screenplay, reaching new heights in the world of sci-fi.
The Zeeka Chronicles is a remarkable contribution to the genre, mixing imagination with powerful themes of survival and human spirit.
ZEEKA AND THE ZOMBIES II (2025) has earned the distinction of becoming a finalist in the 13Horror.com Screenplay Contest 2025, further solidifying its place as a ground-breaking work in both literature and visual media.

SELF-HELP & WRITING GUIDES: EMPOWERING THE NEXT GENERATION OF WRITERS.

Through her self-help books, Brenda shares invaluable knowledge and experience with aspiring authors.
How to Write for Success I, and II (2017, 2021) and Self-Publishing Tips (2022) provide practical advice for budding authors, helping them navigate the complexities of the writing and publishing world.

POETRY ANTHOLOGIES AND MAGAZINES: Amplifying Voices for Change

Brenda has also edited and co-authored poetry anthologies that address vital social issues.
A Spark of Hope I, II, and III (2019–2023) and Break the Silence I, II, and III (2020–2025) tackle topics such as suicide prevention, domestic violence, human trafficking, and addiction.
Peace Begins with Us (2022) and Creating a Better World (2022) encourage readers to take action for positive change.
CIESART Humming Bird Magazines I, II, III, and IV, and How to Write for Success, Magazines I, II, III, IV, and V contain news

articles, poetry, and relevant issues for World Literature.
Check out her pages on her Website.
https://brenchristo.com

COPYRIGHT NOTICE

ZEEKA'S GHOST: REVENGE OF ZEEKA
Published by Brenda Mohammed

www.ingramcontent.com/pod-product-compliance
Lightning Source LLC
LaVergne TN
LVHW031344150826
845673LV00009B/2858

* 9 7 8 1 5 4 2 9 7 7 9 8 2 *